John Henry

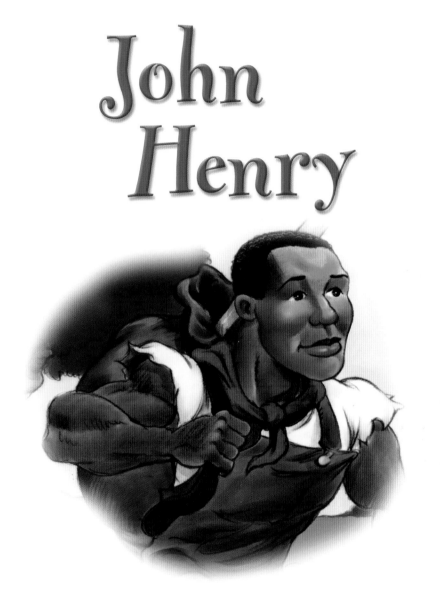

retold by Carol Ottolenghi   illustrated by Steve Haefele

ho was John Henry? Well, folks say that the day John Henry was born the winds howled and the storm clouds gathered so thick that they were pushing each other for space in the sky. People say it was as if the storm was trying to give its power to that little baby.

"This baby's something special!" John Henry's Ma yelled over the booming thunder.

"Every baby's something special," his Pa yelled back.

He fussed over John Henry the way folks always fuss over a baby. Suddenly, little John Henry grabbed the hammer hanging from Pa's belt.

"Jumpin' Jehosephat!" Pa laughed. "This baby was born with a hammer in his hand!"

As a young boy, John Henry learned how to plow fields and pick cotton. But what he really loved to do was hammer with his Pa's old hammer. Why, folks say that he'd pluck lightning bolts from the sky and hammer them straight, just for the practice.

One fine morning, John Henry packed up his hammer. "M
Pa," he said. "It's time I saw the world."

He kissed them good-bye and headed down the road. His M
called him back because he'd forgotten his kerchief. After that,
John Henry never took it off because it reminded him of her.

John Henry walked and walked until he found a farmer who needed some help. He dug a thirty-foot deep well, put up a barn, and built twelve tiny chicken houses on account that the chickens each wanted their own house. That was in the morning!

He spent the afternoon rescuing a young girl's cat from a tree. Trouble was, the cat didn't want to be rescued. Every time John Henry got close, it'd scurry up to higher and skinnier branches. But he caught it in the end.

John Henry tromped all over the country. Whenever he reached a farm or town, he'd stop and ask if anyone needed some work to be done.

Dependin' on the season, John Henry plowed and planted or hoed and weeded. He fixed tools and did other blacksmith work. He helped farmers bring in their crops at harvest time. Wherever he worked, folks fed him and gave him a place to lay his head at night.

John Henry enjoyed meeting all different kinds of folks and doing all different kinds of work. But always, always, the work he loved best was hammering. As he fixed a farmer's plow or pounded a cart wheel into shape, he'd sing, "I was born with a hammer in my hand, oh yes. I was born with a hammer in my hand."

Well, John Henry was traveling to another town when he spied a wagon stuck in the mud. The woman trying to push it out was just an itty-bitty thing.

"You're too little to push that wagon loose," John Henry said

"How else am I going to get it out of this mud?" the woman asked. "You're big and strong, but I don't see you using those muscles."

John Henry grabbed the wagon and dragged it from the mud.

"Thank you," said the woman. She held out her hand. "I'm Lucy Ann."

They talked a bit. Lucy Ann wasn't afraid to speak her mind, and she was mighty pretty. John Henry decided that maybe it was time for him to settle down and get married.

*H*e took a job near Lucy Ann's home, working for the railroad. He'd hammer all day, bustin' boulders into gravel for the railroad bed. And as he swung his hammer, John Henry would sing, "I was born with a hammer in my hand, oh yes. I was born with a hammer in my hand."

One day, the foreman called the workers together.

"The crew over by Big Bend has laid track to the mountains," he said. "But they need help opening a tunnel through the mountains. They'll pay you twice as much as this crew does."

"You'll be driving steel spikes through solid rock," the foreman explained. "You've got to be as strong as an ox to drive those spikes straight."

"You can count on me," John Henry said.

John Henry told Lucy Ann about the tunnel that night.
"I was born to help build that tunnel," John Henry said.
"Lucy Ann, I've got to go."

"Of course, you do," Lucy Ann said. "And I'll go with you.
My aunt and uncle live in that part of the country. They're
getting old and could use my help on the farm. We can stay
with them."

John Henry went to Big Bend and followed the train tracks until he found the work crew.

"I'm John Henry. I've come to drive steel," he said.

"John Henry, eh? I've heard of you," said the Big Bend foreman. "You bust boulders fine enough but can you drive a spike into rock?"

"Sure," said John Henry. "Which one of you shakers is gonna' hold the spike for me?"

The crew stared at John Henry's muscles and shook their heads. They were afraid that if John Henry missed the spike, his hammer would flatten the hand that held it for him. Finally, a small, brave man named Little Bull put a spike in place.

WOOSH! went John Henry's hammer. CLING! went the spike. HURRAH! went the crew.

"It went in with one stroke!" said the foreman. "You're hired!"

That summer was hot and drier than a mouthful of sand. Most crews worked as slow as snails but not the Big Bend crew. That's 'cause John Henry drove spikes twice as fast as anyone else. And as he hammered, he'd sing, "I was born with a hammer in my hand, oh yes. I was born with a hammer in my hand."

Everything was going okay until one day, when a salesman brought a newfangled machine to the crew.

"This steam drill can drive spikes faster than anyone," he said.

"Not faster than John Henry," said the foreman.

"I challenge your man to a contest," said the salesman. "If the machine wins, you buy it. If John Henry wins, I'll give it to you."

"I'll do it," said John Henry. "But if I win, the men keep their jobs."

John Henry talked it over with Lucy Ann that night.

"I'm worried," John Henry admitted. "I don't know if I can beat a machine. But if I don't, we all lose our jobs."

"You can only try your best," said Lucy Ann. "Remember—you were born with a hammer in your hand, John Henry. You were born with a hammer in your hand."

The sun was shining so hot the day of the contest that hen
were laying hardboiled eggs. John Henry and Little Bull got th
spikes ready.

The salesman rolled the steam drill into position. He filled th
boiler with water and stoked the fire. Then, he fussed and
fidgeted, pulling levers and pushing buttons. The drill sputterec
coughed up a bunch of black smoke, and started chugging aw

"Start driving!" yelled the foreman.
WOOSH! CLING! went John Henry's hammer.
TAT-TAT-TAT-TAT! went the steam drill.
"The steam drill is ahead!" cried one man.
"No, John Henry is ahead!" yelled another.

At the end of the first hour, John Henry was sweating so much that his hammer kept sliding out of his hands. The steam drill chugged along, but the black smoke it spat out was getting thicker.

"It's ahead of us," John Henry said to Little Bull.

"We'll catch it," said Little Bull.

John Henry picked up his hammer. WOOSH! CLING!

"That's it!" cried Little Bull. "We can catch it!"

But by the end of the second hour, everyone could see that the steam drill was still ahead. The crew was nervous.

"No one drives steel better than John Henry," Lucy Ann said. "If he can't beat that machine, no one can."

And it sure looked like no one could beat that machine.
Black smoke was pouring out of it by the end of the third hour,
but it didn't show any signs of slowing down.

"I can't let the crew down!" yelled John Henry. "I've got to g
faster. Little Bull, get me a second hammer."

Well, John Henry set both his arms a-swinging, and that helped some. By the end of the fourth hour, John Henry had gained on the steam drill. But he and Little Bull were still behind.

WOOSH! CLING! WOOSH! CLING! went John Henry's two hammers.

TAT-TAT-TAT-TAT! went the steam drill.

"I've never seen a man use two hammers before," cried one ma

"John Henry is no ordinary man," said Lucy Ann.

At the end of the fifth hour, the sun was shining straight overhead. Folks were eating picnic lunches or taking naps in the shade. But John Henry and the steam drill kept right on going.

By the sixth hour of the contest, John Henry was plum tuckered out. Worse, the steam drill was still ahead. So, John Henry thought about how much he and the men needed their jobs. He thought about how everyone believed in him. He started humming and swinging his hammers faster, keepin' time with the music.

TAT-TAT-TAT-TAT! went the steam drill.

"He's almost caught the machine!" someone yelled.

"Go, John Henry, go!" cheered the crowd.

John Henry didn't hear the crowd or the steam drill. All he heard was the song he was humming, "I was born with a hammer in my hand, oh yes. I was born with a hammer in my hand."

When John Henry passed the machine, the crowd whooped and hollered something fierce.

Suddenly, the steam drill started to sputter. Something exploded, and there was a huge cloud of black smoke. The salesman ran for a bucket of water.

WOOSH! CLING! WOOSH! CLING! went John Henry's hammers. He kept right on going, even though the machine had stopped.

The salesman dumped bucket after bucket of water on the steam drill, trying to cool it off so that it would start again. And all that time, John Henry never stopped. WOOSH! CLING! WOOSH! CLING!

Finally, after two hours, the steam drill started. John Henry was a good five feet ahead, and there was only one hour left in the contest.

"Time's up!" yelled the foreman.

John Henry dropped right where he stood. The foreman measured the hole that John Henry had dug. He measured the hole the steam drill had dug.

"The steam drill went nine feet into the mountain," he said. "Now, that's pretty impressive. But John Henry," the foreman looked around and smiled, "John Henry dug fifteen feet!"

Folks threw their hats in the air and cheered.

John Henry never heard the cheers. He had hammered so hard and so fast that his heart burst in his chest.

They buried John Henry on the hillside overlooking the tunnel that he helped to dig. Folks say that if you listen closely, you can hear the wind whispering, "I was born with a hammer in my hand, oh yes. I was born with a hammer in my hand."

Is This Story True?

Some of it is! The tunnel is real, although it isn't used anymore. It was built in West Virginia in the 1870s. At that time, it was the longest tunnel in the world. The steam drill was first used around this time as well. And it's quite possible that there was a former slave named John Henry who worked on building the railroad. But the contest and other feats that folks say happened are probably just part of the legend that surrounds John Henry.

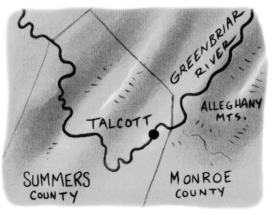